Dedicated to:
Miss Frickey, my first-grade teacher in Syracuse,
New York, who discovered and nurtured my love
for drawing pictures.
Herr Kraus, my art teacher in *Gymnasium*,
high school, in Stuttgart, Germany, who introduced
me to modern art when it was forbidden to be shown.
Professor Schneidler, who inspired me when I studied
graphic design under him at the *Akademie der
Bildenden Künste*, Stuttgart.

The author and publisher thank Dr Marianne Torbert,
Director, The Leonard Gorden Institute for
Human Development Through Play, Temple University,
Philadelphia, Pennsylvania, for her comments.

Ann Beneduce, consulting editor

PUFFIN BOOKS

UK | USA | Canada | Ireland | Australia | India | New Zealand | South Africa

Puffin Books is part of the Penguin Random House group of companies
whose addresses can be found at global.penguinrandomhouse.com.

www.penguin.co.uk   www.puffin.co.uk   www.ladybird.co.uk

Penguin
Random House
UK

First published in the United States of America by HarperCollins 1997
First published in Great Britain by Hamish Hamilton Ltd 1998
Published in Puffin Books 1999
Reissued 2018

002

Printed in China

A CIP catalogue record for this book is available from the British Library

ISBN: 978–0–140–56378–8

All correspondence to:
Puffin Books
Penguin Random House Children's
80 Strand, London WC2R 0RL

FSC
www.fsc.org

MIX
Paper from
responsible sources
FSC® C018179

Eric Carle
From Head
to Toe

PUFFIN

I am a penguin
and I turn my head.
Can you do it?

I can do it!

I am a giraffe
and I bend my neck.
Can you do it?

I can do it!

I am a buffalo
and I raise my shoulders.
Can you do it?

I can do it!

I am a monkey
and I wave my arms.
	Can you do it?

I am a seal
and I clap my hands.
Can you do it?

I can do it!

I am a gorilla
and I thump my chest.
Can you do it?

I can do it!

I am a cat
and I arch my back.
Can you do it?

I can do it!

I am a crocodile
and I wriggle my hips.
Can you do it?

I can do it!

I am a camel
and I bend my knees.
         Can you do it?

I can do it!

I am a donkey
and I kick my legs.
Can you do it?

I can do it!

I am an elephant
and I stomp my foot.
        Can you do it?

I can do it!

I am I
and I wiggle my toe.
    Can you do it?

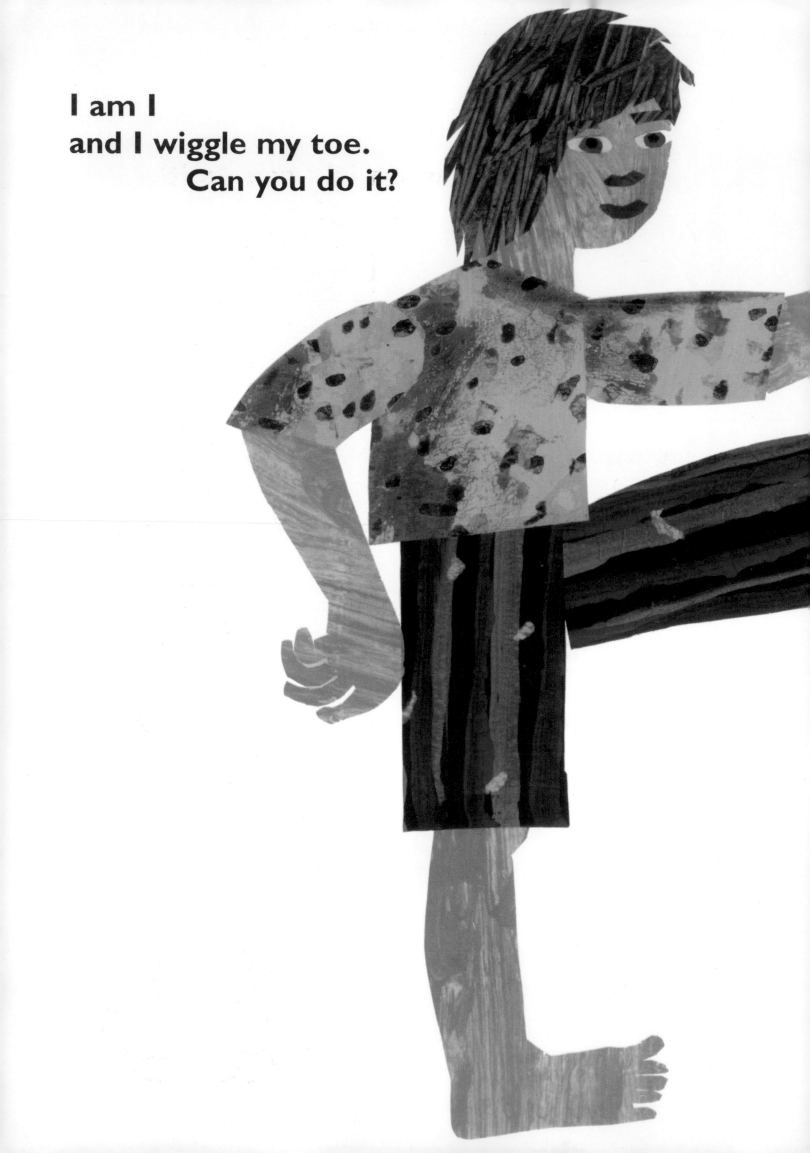

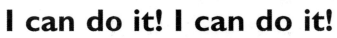

I can do it! I can do it!

"The joy and celebration of learning and growing are always a part of Eric Carle's books. **From Head to Toe** is no exception, but is perhaps exceptional in the added dimension of literally 'moving' through this book. Not only can children listen, imagine, discover, feel, and think, but now they can also be a part of the action. It is as if Eric Carle has again reached out and in his special way said, 'Come play with me.'"

Dr. Marianne Torbert, Director
The Leonard Gordon Institute for Human
Development Through Play
Temple University, Philadelphia, PA 19122

About this book, Eric Carle says: "Just as alphabet books introduce the very young child to letters and simple words, **From Head to Toe**, through a playful and rhythmic question-and-answer word game, introduces that same child to the basic body parts and simple body movements.

"And in the same way that a child progresses from understanding simple words to reading and writing more complex words, sentences and stories, so he or she will progress from making simple body movements to dancing, doing exercises, performing gymnastics, and participating with confidence and pleasure in sports and other activities."